Vroomaloom Zoom

by John Coy

illustrated by Joe Cepeda

Crown Publishers

New York

For my mother
—John Coy

For the students at Humphreys Avenue
School in East Los Angeles
—Joe Cepeda

Text copyright © 2000 by John Coy
Illustrations copyright © 2000 by Joe Cepeda

Published by Crown Publishers, a division of Random House, Inc., 1540 Broadway, New York, New York 10036.

CROWN and colophon are trademarks of Random House, Inc.

www.randomhouse.com/kids

Library of Congress Cataloging-in-Publication Data
Coy, John, 1958– .
Vroomaloom zoom / by John Coy ; illustrated by Joe Cepeda.—1st ed.
p.   cm.
Summary: Daddy takes Carmela on an imaginary car ride, lulling her to sleep with various sounds, from the wurgle lurgle of swamps to the hoopty doopty swoopty loopty of driving in circles.
ISBN 0-517-80009-8 (trade) — ISBN 0-517-80010-1 (lib. bdg.)
[1. Sound—Fiction. 2. Automobile travel—Fiction. 3. Imagination—Fiction. 4. Bedtime—Fiction.]   I. Cepeda, Joe, ill. II. Title.
PZ7.C839455 Vr 2000
[E]—dc21   99-462103

First Edition • Printed in the United States of America • October 2000

10 9 8 7 6 5 4 3 2 1

One August evening,
cake-bake hot,
Carmela and her dad decide on a ride.
"Bring your blankie." Dad grabs the keys.
Carmela buckles up in the big yellow car.

Vroomaloom zoomaloom vroom zoom.

"Ready for sleep?" Dad says as they drive out of town.
"Not yet, Daddy. Keep driving."
So they drive past farms

cackle lackle

through woods
whoo whoo

in cities

pell mell bell YELL

all the way to the sea

splash
dash wave CRASH.

"Ready?"
"Not yet, Daddy. Keep driving."

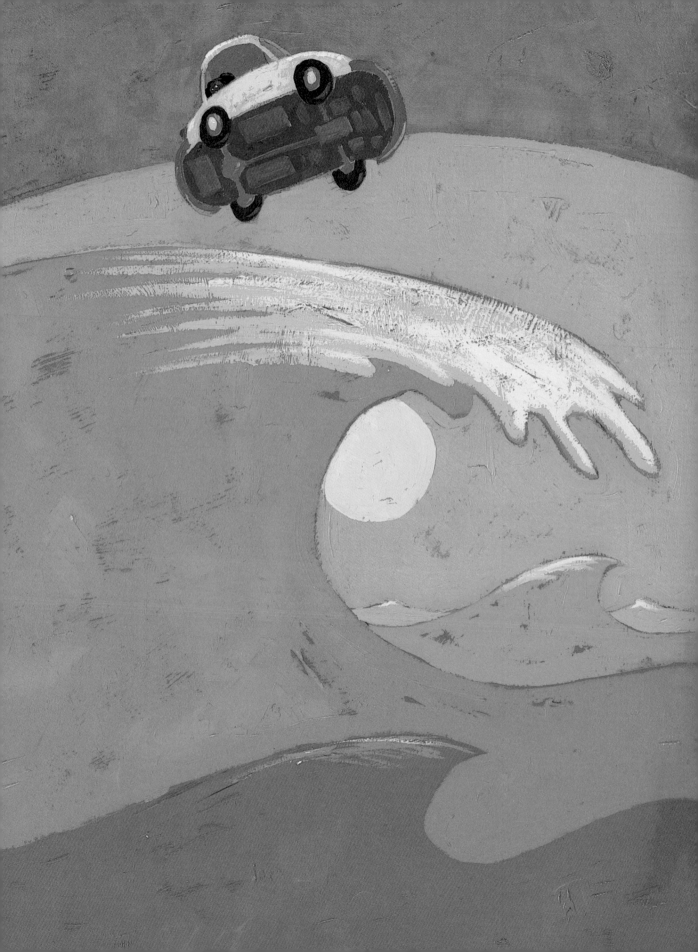

So they drive across swamps

wurgle lurgle

over streams

pip o lip
dip o lip

up mountains

hip

hop

tippy top

and around waterfalls

rdrd rdrd rd rd rd.

"Ready?"
"Not yet, Daddy. Keep driving."

So they drive forward

SWOOSH AWOOSH

backward

BE DEEP BE DEEP

sideways

jig jag zig zag

and around in circles

hoopty doopty
swoopty loopty.

Carmela's eyes close as she snuggles in her sea

Zzzmmm.

"Now you're ready," Dad whispers.

She pops open an eye.

"Not yet, Daddy. Keep driving."

Vroomaloom
   zoomaloom
 vroom
   zoom.